Performance

ILLUSTRATED BY JAN LEWIS

Can you help me read this at home?

Are we all going to be in the play?

Does anyone know the story of Aladdin?

Can I have one? Will there be a part for me?

Let's use the music on this CD. The piano's loud!

Who has done a painting of the genie?

Where shall we put the poster? On the wall?

How many rehearsals will there be?

I can't wave and stand on one leg! Can you?

Shall I stop the music? Is it too loud?

We need lots of practice! Let's start again.

Stop! I've dropped my flag! Keep on dancing.

Sing up! Reach for those high notes!

Stand here. We'll read the words together.

She's good! What part is she playing?

Oh, where did you come from?

There's a lot of scenery to paint! I'm tired!

What jobs still need to be done? Can I help?

The magic lamp will be lovely. We'll paint it gold.

Can we decorate it with this jewel I made?

How many instruments are there? Can I play one?

Who has heard any of these before?

Take it in turn to try them out.

Do we shake, blow or bang them?

I'm really tangled up with my turban! It's so long!

That's perfect! Now try it by yourself. Keep it tight.

Could we use this cloth in the play?

Stand still! Shall I tie a knot or a bow?

This face paint is hard to do! Do you need help?

This costume makes me look really scary!

Roll up, roll up! How many tickets would you like?

Read all about the show in this booklet!

Who has family or friends in the audience?

I'm nervous now. What if I forget my words?

I have a script. I can prompt you.

Is everyone in the right place? Good luck!

I'll give this old lamp a polish. That's better.

Surprise, Aladdin! I am the genie of the lamp.

Who's this at the door? What's he selling?

New lamps for old! Let's swap!

And they all lived happily ever after!

Oops! My beard has fallen off again!